RIPLEY'S WORLD

Written by
Connie Herrick

Illustrated by
Mark Herrick

ISBN Hardcover: 978-1-7376514-0-6
ISBN Paperback: 978-1-7376514-1-3
ISBN eBook: 978-1-7376514-2-0

Library of Congress Control Number: 2021915015

First hardcover edition 2021

DESIGN: PIPER MURAKAMI
COPY EDITOR: DOUGLAS JACKSON

RipleysWorld.com

Our book was joyfully created
with deep love for our
wonderful son Matt,
our four-legged and fish family...
and of course Ripley.

At this very moment, in a small town not so far from here, is a tiny, friendly, calico kitty named Ripley.

She is feisty, funny and full of ideas. Ripley is mostly white with patches of black and butterscotch.

Not too long ago, Ripley's two-legged family was out driving in their car. As they passed the local animal shelter, an unusual feeling came over them.

So, they stopped the car, turned around
and went back to the shelter. There, they
found tiny Ripley, waiting and hoping
for a special family to take her home.

She was so small — she could fit in the palm
of your hand! But within a few minutes,
it became clear that inside this teeny little
kitty was a huge personality.

It was love at first sight for everyone.
Sometimes, things are just meant to be.

Ripley lives in a happy house with a small backyard garden. She starts every day with a morning stroll. "I love to watch the bees and hummingbirds zip all around my garden," says Ripley.

"Look at all the colorful flowers! Blue wisteria, yellow orchids, red camellias, purple sage and pink crabapple blossoms," she happily trills.

"Follow me!" says Ripley. "It's time to wake up my family and get them to fix me breakfast. I'm hungry! Aren't you?"

"I love, love, love to wake up early.
First, I stretch and yawn. Next,
I wash my face and clean my toe beans.
I always keep my nose and toe beans
nice and pink."

"Then, I wake up my two-legged family.
I have a very special way to get them
out of bed. It works every time!"

"I call it 'Nose and Toes,'" says Ripley
with a gleam in her eye.

"First, I bite their nose."

"If that doesn't wake them up,
then I bite their toes! Hee-hee!"

With her two-legged family wide awake and fixing her breakfast, Ripley stops at the fish tank for a good morning visit. "I love my fish family because they come in all different shapes, sizes and colors."

"Swimming together, they shimmer like a beautiful underwater rainbow," she says.

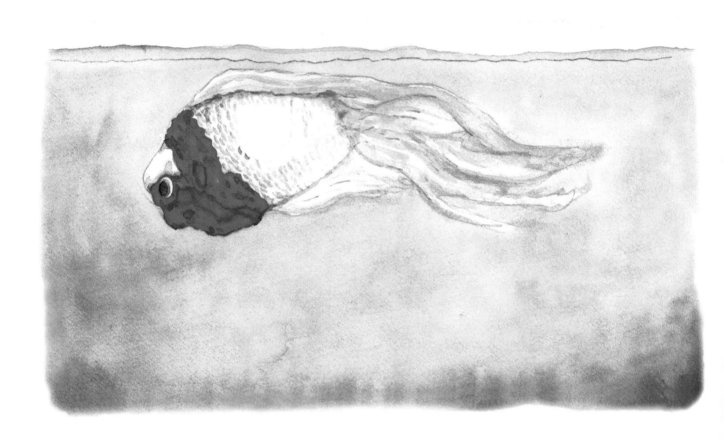

"This is my little brother Hariel," says Ripley. "He is very special because he swims upside down all the time."

Hariel is sparkly white with a bright orange head and polka dot fins. He can swim faster than all the other fish and loves to make big splashes. Somersaults are his specialty.

"I like to tickle his belly and make Hariel laugh bubbles!" giggles Ripley.

"Hey Hariel – look at me! I'm ready to scuba and do somersaults with you!"

Pretending to be a scuba diver is one of Ripley's favorite things to do. She loves the wavy water and twinkly bubbles.

"Meet my two smelly German Shepherd sisters," laughs Ripley. "Pele is the older one. She is big and her bark is very loud. Kapo is the younger one. She is smaller than Pele, but her bark is just as loud."

Pele is a search and rescue dog. She went
to a special school so that she could learn
how to find people who are lost. Her nose is
very strong. She can smell things that are
far away or hidden. She is very smart, very
calm and very good at her job.

Kapo's nose is also very special.

She can smell the tiniest of smells.

With her sensitive nose, she can follow

the footsteps of a lost person.

She is fast,   full of energy and can

can chase   a ball all day long.

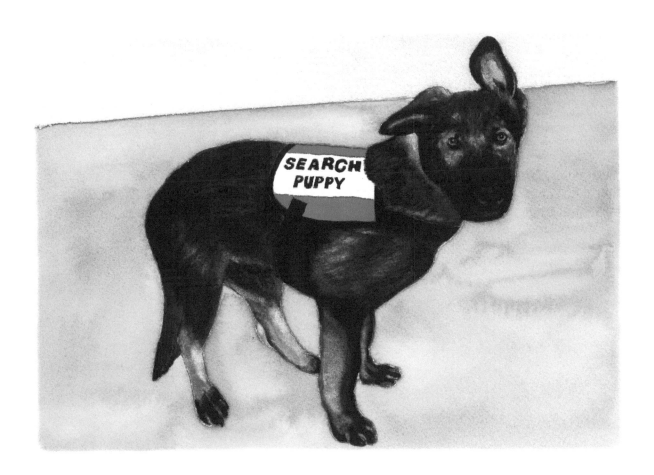

"When I get older, I want to be a search and rescue dog just like my sister, Pele," says Kapo.

She loves to wear her training vest and practice finding people. Kapo is also very smart, but not very calm.

"Good morning Pele! You're eating breakfast awfully fast. Are you doing search and rescue work today?" asks Ripley.

"Yes! We just got a call to go look for a lost person. I've got to get my uniform on and go find them. I'll tell you all about it when I get home. Bye for now!" says Pele.

"Kapo eats breakfast really fast like Pele, but that's just how she is with lunch and dinner too," laughs Ripley.

"Sometimes, she is silly and tries to eat right out of the food bin!"

"It's time to find out what my friends are up to," thinks Ripley. She heads outside and climbs up onto the top of the fence.

Behind her backyard fence is a very green, very thick, very tall Bamboo Forest. This is where her friends live.

"Helloooo! Anybody in there?" calls Ripley as she sticks her head into the bamboo leaves. "Come out, come out! It's time to play!"

Ripley loves her Bamboo Forest friends.
Almost every day, she plays with
Nash, the squirrel, and the raccoon
twins, Mathilde and Christopher.
Ripley likes to call the twins "Mattie"
and "Topher."

There is much running, jumping, chasing
and laughing!

Nash, the red-tailed squirrel shoots out of
the Bamboo Forest and scampers toward
Ripley. "Good morning Nash!" says Ripley.

"Howdy Ripley! Let's play
Touch Nose Tag. Catch me
if you can," laughs Nash.
"Tag! You're it!"

Touch Nose Tag is one of Ripley's favorite games. Nash is an extremely fast runner and tends to win most of the time.

"Today I will catch him!" squeals Ripley.

"Not today or any day!" yells Nash as he darts off at light speed, so fast he looks like a blur of red fur and little feet!

When playtime is over, a very tired Ripley goes inside for a nap in her special napping place. It has just the right amount of sun and a view of the Bamboo Forest.

She shares it with her five soft, comfy napping babies. "I love my babies," she purrs.

When Ripley wakes up, Nash says, "Hurry up sleepyhead! Mattie and Topher are here for a visit." The raccoon twins look alike, but they have very different personalities.

Mattie loves gymnastics and is constantly tumbling, climbing up trees and swinging from branches. Her dream is to be a trapeze artist flying high above the ground.

Topher is very prim and proper and prefers to stay close to the ground. He doesn't like to get dirty and is careful to wash everything he eats at least three times.

"What are those two are up to today?" wonders Ripley.

Uh oh! Looks like Mattie and Topher
are in a spot of trouble.

"Don't worry Ripley! We are pretending
to be acrobats on a trapeze but the
branch is too skinny to hold the both
of us," shouts Mattie.

Topher is not happy. He is high up
a tree and now has tree sap all over
his fur. He will have to wash himself
many, many times to get it all off.

Mama P and her three little possums, Pax, Pili and Paisley, are out for their daily afternoon walk. "What is that ahead? Oh no! It's Mattie and Topher hanging from a branch!" gasps Mama P.

"Oh my goodness! That branch is way too thin to hold you both. Please get down carefully before you get hurt!"

She waits to make sure Mattie and Topher are safely back on the ground. "Those two and their tree shenanigans. Acrobats indeed," says Mama P to herself.

While Mama P watches Mattie and Topher
get down from the tree safely, Pax, Pili
and Paisley scamper up and find a very thin
branch they can wrap their tails around.

"Look at us Mama! We're acrobats on a trapeze too," says Pax. "Oh my goodness!" says Mama P as she runs up the tree and gets her three Ps safely off the branch.

Oh no! Now Ripley is in the same spot of trouble. The spot is so big now, it's a puddle of trouble! Everyone wants to be an acrobat today.

"Oh my goodness!" says Mama P as she runs up the tree to get Ripley safely down off the branch.

"Thank you Mama P for getting me back on the ground!" says Ripley.

"Three 'Oh my goodnesses' in one day. I need a nap," says Mama P to herself.

Suddenly, there is a lot of noise and activity buzzing through the house.

"Ripley! Ripley! Hurry up and come quick! Pele is home from her search!" shouts Kapo.

Ripley and Kapo rush to greet Pele. They are so excited to hear all about her search adventure.

"We found the lost person. They took a wrong turn off a hiking trail and couldn't find their way back. Luckily, they weren't hurt and we found them quickly," says Pele.

"And after the search, we got to do a special helicopter training! I went for a ride and flew all around. It was so loud but tons of fun!"

Dinnertime! Ripley, Mattie and Topher
are very, very hungry after their big tree
adventure. They all dive in and eat until
their tummies are full. Fresh figs, apples
and plums from the backyard garden make
a delicious meal for the twin raccoons.
Crunch, crunch, crunch!

Does anyone want some of my Krunchy
Kibble Bits and Salmon Snax?" asks Ripley.
She hopes not, because she's very hungry.
Ripley loves eating dinner with her friends.
Everyone has round little bellies and
satisfied smiles.

What an exciting day! There is even
a special dessert treat to celebrate
Pele finding the lost person. Vanilla
ice cream! Yum!

After dinner, Ripley's favorite show
America's Funniest Cats is on TV. "I love to
watch the kitties doing funny, silly things!"
giggles Ripley. She laughs and laughs.

There is still a little time left before bedtime for Ripley to play one quick game of *Grab the Guppy* on her iPad.

She is very fast, but no matter how hard she tries, she can never catch the quick little fish.

"That's okay," thinks Ripley. "I'll try again tomorrow. Someday I'll catch that clever little guppy."

It was a very, very good day filled
with fun, laughter and much excitement.
With Pele home safe, the lost person
found and the moon and stars shining
in the night sky, it is finally bedtime.

Good night and sweet dreams,
Pele and Kapo.

Good night and sweet dreams, Hariel.

Good night and sweet dreams,
Mattie and Topher.

Good night and sweet dreams, Nash.

Good night and sweet dreams,
Pax, Pili, Paisley and Mama P.

Ripley's last thought as she drifts off
to sleep is how grateful she is to have
a loving family, wonderful friends,
a soft bed, food to eat, a beautiful
Bamboo Forest and another fun-filled
day on the horizon.

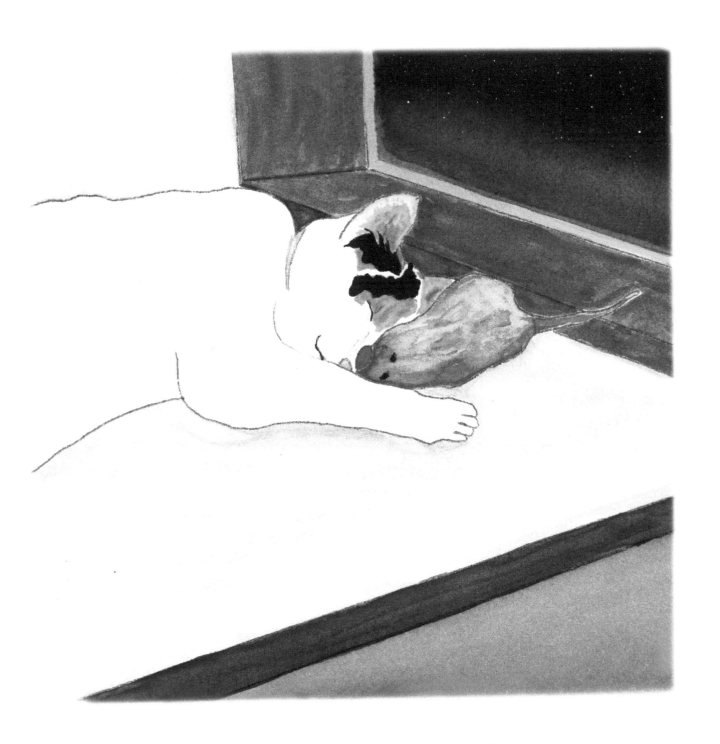

Good night and sweet dreams, Ripley.

Good night and sweet dreams, dear reader.

Ripley will be waiting for you to join her and her friends for more adventures, more laughter and more fun!

(Not) The End

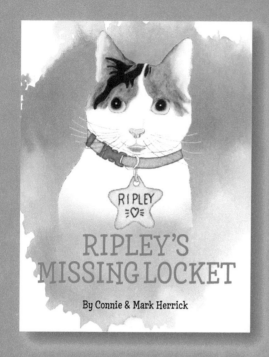

RIPLEY'S
MISSING LOCKET

By Connie & Mark Herrick

Here's a sneak peek at Ripley's next exciting adventure: Ripley's Missing Locket. Join Ripley, her family and her friends as they search her house, backyard, the Bamboo Forest and the neighborhood community garden for her missing locket!

"I'll search high and low. First, I'll go high,"
thought Ripley. She made a quick jump
up onto the kitchen counter and carefully
climbed onto the top of the toaster oven.
She was very, very high up. Standing on
her tippy toes, she slowly pulled open the
cabinet door and peeked inside.

A Message from
Ripley's Two-legged Family

Ripley was part of our family for 18 years.
Our sweet kitty with the pinkest little toe beans had a
zest for life, an incredible imagination and a deep love
of empty boxes and computer keyboards.

She was to us exactly as portrayed in our book.
The inspiration for most of the watercolor illustrations
came from our family photo albums. Our family spent
many happy hours watching her play with the squirrels,
raccoons and possums in our backyard.

Pele, Kapo, Hariel and the fishies were all
members of our family too. Pele and Kapo were search
and rescue dogs for 12 years. They found and rescued
many missing people. Hariel, our oranda goldfish, had a
swim bladder defect which is why he could only swim
upside down. He lived that way for 10 years.

Kapo is still with us. While retired now from search
and rescue, she can still chase the ball all day long.

– CONNIE & MARK HERRICK